When I Have a Little Girl

by
Charlotte Zolotow

Pictures by
Hilary Knight

Harper & Row, Publishers
New York

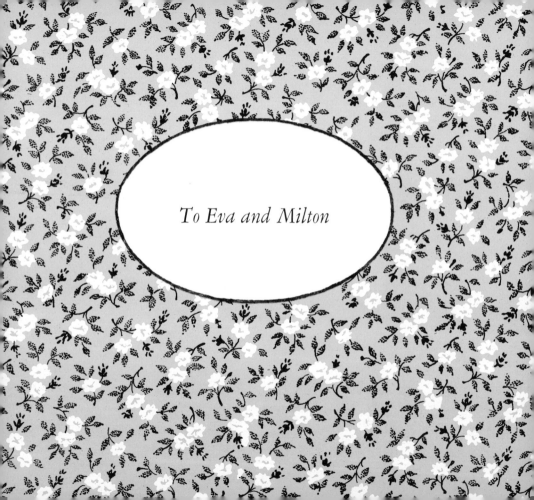

To Eva and Milton

When I have a little girl . . .

She can wear party dresses to school.

She can be fresh to unpleasant people.

She can go through all my bureau drawers . . .

and try on rings and bracelets and scarves without asking.

She can have a party every week . . .

and go to a restaurant once a month
and order whatever she wants.

She can go without a coat or hat or boots . . .

the very first warm day . . .

even if it snows again later.

She can let her hair grow . . . .

. . . . as long as she wants.

She can have a friend stay overnight whenever she wants.

And one bath a week will be enough.

And nobody will tell her in winter
to stop eating snow.

Or in summer to come out of the ocean
even if she is turning blue.

She can touch the fur collars of ladies
in front of her on the bus or train . . .

or standing in line.

And she can pat any dog she wants
without asking if it's friendly.
(She'll know. I always do.)

She can tell anything
she wants about me
to anyone she wants.

She can always answer the phone
and talk first to anyone who calls
even if it's business.

She can have a new box
of crayons every week even if
the older ones are still good
and just not pointed anymore.

^{S}he can uncover the leaves around the crocus shoots and then cover them up if it should snow again.

She won't have to be home
before dark, so she will be able
to see the moon rise.

And she can get up in the morning before it's light and go out in her nightgown to watch the sun come up.

She can give milk to all the cats
and if they don't go away afterward . . .

they can live with her.

When I have a little girl
all the rules will be
different.

And I will never
say to her,
"When you are a mother
you will understand
why all these rules
are necessary."

My mother says . . .

her mother used to say it too.